# Anya
## the Cuddly Creatures Fairy

Special thanks to
Rachel Elliot

ORCHARD BOOKS
338 Euston Road, London NW1 3BH
Orchard Books Australia
Level 17/207 Kent Street, Sydney, NSW 2000
A Paperback Original

First published in 2011 by Orchard Books

© 2011 Rainbow Magic Limited.
A HIT Entertainment company. Rainbow Magic
is a trademark of Rainbow Magic Limited.
Reg. U.S. Pat. & Tm. Off. And other countries.
www.rainbowmagiconline.com

HiT entertainment

Illustrations © Orchard Books 2011

A CIP catalogue record for this book is available
from the British Library.

ISBN 978 1 40831 295 7

5 7 9 10 8 6

Printed in Great Britain

The paper and board used in this paperback are natural recyclable
products made from wood grown in sustainable forests. The
manufacturing processes conform to the environmental regulations
of the country of origin.

Orchard Books is a division of Hachette Children's Books,
an Hachette UK company

www.hachette.co.uk

# Anya
## the Cuddly Creatures
## Fairy

by Daisy Meadows

ORCHARD

www.rainbowmagic.co.uk

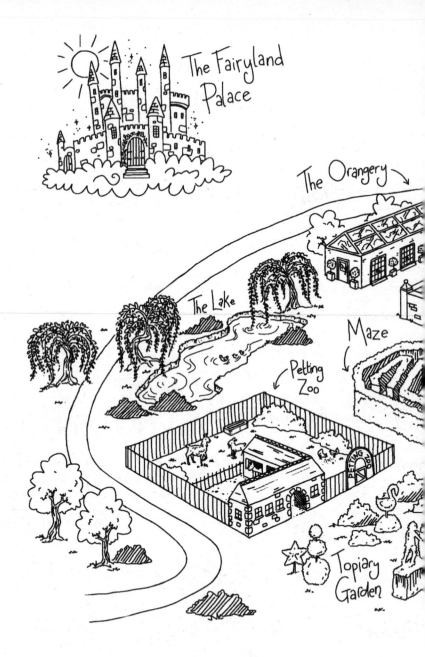

The Fairyland
Palace

The Orangery

The Lake

Maze

Petting
Zoo

PETTING ZOO

Topiary
Garden

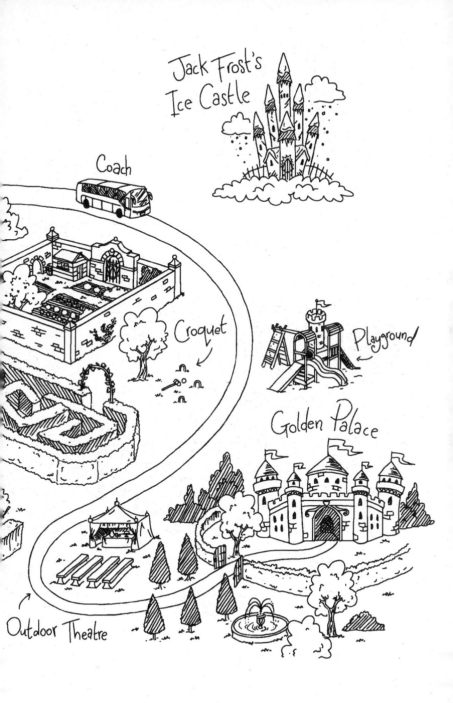

Jack Frost's
Ice Castle

Coach

Croquet

Playground

Golden Palace

Outdoor Theatre

The fairies are planning a magical ball,
With guests of honour and fun for them all.
They're expecting a night full of laughter and cheer
But they'll get a shock when my goblins appear!

Adventures and treats will be things of the past,
And I'll beat those troublesome fairies at last.
My iciest magic will blast through the room
And the world will be plunged into grimness
and gloom!

# Contents

# Sunshine at Golden Palace

"Another perfect day!" said Rachel Walker happily. She was standing in the sunshine on the grand entrance steps of Golden Palace. Rachel's, best friend, Kirsty Tate looked up at the sky and smiled as the bright sunbeams warmed her face.

"It's royal weather for a royal palace!" Kirsty agreed.

Kirsty and Rachel were staying at Golden Palace for a special Kids' Week over the spring holidays. Today, Kirsty's mother was bringing Kirsty's little cousin Charlie to spend the day with them.

"I'm looking forward to showing Charlie all the amazing places here," said Kirsty. "I wonder what he'll like best. The drawbridge? The moat?"

"Or the petting zoo, or the magic

staircases, or the dungeons, or the maze," said Rachel, counting them off on her fingers. "There are so many things to show him, I don't think a day will be long enough!"

"Staying here really does make me feel like a princess," Kirsty said, gazing out across the palace gardens.

"How about a Princess Fairy?" Rachel asked.

The girls shared a secret smile. They were friends with the fairies who lived in Fairyland, and they often helped them when Jack Frost and his naughty goblins caused trouble. At the moment, the fairies needed their help more than ever before. When the girls had arrived at Golden Palace, they had been invited to a special ball in Fairyland in honour of the Princess Fairies. But Jack Frost had gatecrashed the party and stolen the princesses' tiaras!

"Jack Frost is so mean," said Kirsty, thinking about the cold-hearted master of the Ice Castle. "The Princess Fairies need their tiaras to make sure that humans and fairies have a happy, magical time. Without them, there will be problems all over the human world and Fairyland."

"We've already found two of the tiaras," Rachel reminded her best friend. "And we know

that the others are somewhere at Golden Palace. I'm sure we'll find them!"

Queen Titania hadn't been able to stop Jack Frost taking the tiaras to the human world but she had cast a spell to make sure that they would be at Golden Palace, so the girls could help to get them back.

Before the girls could say another word about Fairyland or the tiaras, they saw Mrs Tate's car gliding over the drawbridge and pulling up in front of the palace.

"Hi, Mum!" called Kirsty, waving. "Hi, Charlie!"

A very excited-looking little boy clambered out of the car.

"Hi, Kirsty!" he called at the top
of his voice. "Hi, Rachel! This is an
AMAZING place!"

Mrs Tate hugged Kirsty and Rachel.

"Are you enjoying yourselves, girls?"
she asked.

"Oh yes!" Rachel exclaimed. "It's
even more exciting here than we
expected!"

"We want to
show Charlie
the
petting
zoo and
the royal
stables,"
said
Kirsty
eagerly.

At that moment, Mrs Tate gave a cry. One of the palace peacocks had jumped up onto a pillar and started pecking at her handbag!

"Shoo!" said Rachel, flapping her arms at the peacock.

The peacock lifted its tail feathers and stalked away indignantly. Kirsty and Rachel stared after it in astonishment.

"I've never seen a peacock act like that before!" said Kirsty, frowning.

"Me neither," Rachel added.

"Perhaps there's something in the air," said Mrs Tate. "Kirsty's cat, Pearl, has been behaving oddly too. She's been running away and hiding all morning."

"That's really strange," said Kirsty, frowning. "Pearl usually loves curling up in people's laps."

"Perhaps she's missing you," said Charlie.

"I wonder if Buttons is missing *me*," said Rachel, thinking of her shaggy dog.

"I'm sure he is," said Mrs Tate. "I must be going now, but I'll be back to pick you up this afternoon, Charlie. Bye, girls!"

She got into her car and waved her hand out of the window as she drove away.

When the car had disappeared over the drawbridge, Kirsty turned to Charlie with a big smile.

"What would you like to see first, Charlie," she said, "the maze or the petting zoo?"

"Oooh, I want to see the animals!" said Charlie, his eyes shining with delight. "I love animals!"

# Pony
# Pandemonium

Rachel and Kirsty led Charlie round to the playground behind the palace. Charlie gasped when he saw the tall climbing frame in the centre.

"That's called Rapunzel's Tower," Rachel explained.

"I'm definitely having a go on that later!" Charlie declared.

They passed the Snow White Wendy house, walked around the lake and at last reached the little petting zoo. Charlie smiled happily when he saw the pig pen, the goat enclosure and the rabbit hutches.

Rachel crouched down beside a fluffy white lop-eared rabbit. She saw a little bucket full of salad scraps, and picked out some lettuce for the rabbit.

"Would you like to feed him?" she asked Charlie.

Charlie crouched down beside her and held out the lettuce. But the rabbit turned around and hopped away!

Charlie's smile faded a little.

"Did I do something wrong?" he asked.

"Maybe he's not feeling very well," Kirsty suggested. "Perhaps we should tell Jean, the animal keeper."

She looked around for the keeper, but the only people in sight were five boys who were peering into the hen house. They were wearing jodhpurs and smart riding jackets, with long riding boots and velvety riding hats. The brims of the hats hid their faces completely.

"No eggs in here!" one of the boys
yelled across.

Then Kirsty noticed something that
seemed very strange.

"Rachel, look!" she said. "There are
guinea pigs on top of the hen house!"

Sure enough, several guinea pigs were
now sitting on the hen house roof. Kirsty
and Rachel exchanged surprised glances.

Meanwhile, the boys had moved over to the rabbit hutches, and were trying to stroke the rabbits. But every time they got close, the rabbits scattered.

"Come on," said Kirsty, seeing that Charlie was disappointed.  "Let's visit the royal stables."

The girls led the way to the royal stable yard. They were surprised to see a beautiful golden carriage standing on the cobbles. In the sunshine the gold sparkled and glimmered like fairy dust.

Kirsty and Rachel peeped inside the carriage and saw soft red plush seats and wide padded armrests.

"It looks magical," Rachel whispered in delight.

"Just like Cinderella's carriage," said Kirsty, smiling at her best friend.

Charlie was looking at some sacks of animal feed standing against the wall.

"Horse oats, hen maize and llama grain," he said, reading the labels aloud. "Each animal has its own special food."

Suddenly they heard a loud neighing and stamping.

"It's coming from that stall over there!" said Rachel, looking round. "Come on!"

The girls and Charlie raced over to the stall, which had a brass plaque on the door:

**My name is Duchess.**
**I am a Shetland pony.**

Charlie and the girls peered in through the stable door. Inside, Jean the animal keeper was standing beside a pretty Shetland pony, holding a grooming brush.

"Calm down, Duchess," Jean was saying. "I'm only trying to make you look your best."

"Hello, Jean!" said Rachel. "We've come to show Charlie around the stables."

"I love ponies," said Charlie, running into the stable.

"Be careful!" warned Jean. "Duchess is in a very funny mood this morning."

Just then, Duchess gave a loud snort and broke away from Jean.

She dashed past Charlie, knocking him
into a pile of straw, and charged out into
the cobbled yard.

"Duchess, stop!" Jean cried.

But Duchess was in a
bad temper, and
she wasn't
listening.
She
kicked
over the
sacks
that were
stacked
against the
wall, and grain,
maize and oats poured out across the
cobbles of the yard.

"Oh, *Duchess!*" exclaimed Jean.

Charlie hid nervously behind Kirsty while Jean coaxed Duchess back into her stable and Rachel picked up the toppled sacks. At last Jean came out and closed the stable door behind her.

"I don't know what's wrong with Duchess," she said. "She's usually such a friendly little pony. Today's Kids' Week activity is taking place here later – I hope she's in a better mood by then."

Rachel and Kirsty exchanged glances, both thinking the same thing. So many animals had been acting strangely this morning – could it possibly have something to do with the Princess Fairies' missing tiaras?

# Anya Appears!

Jean scooped some feed into a bucket and smiled at Charlie, who looked upset.

"Are you OK after your tumble in the straw?" Jean said, ruffling Charlie's hair. "I'm sorry about Duchess. Would you like to come and help me feed some of the other animals?"

"Yes, please!" cried Charlie excitedly.

"Perhaps you can try to get the guinea pigs to come down from the hen house," Jean added. "They've been up there all morning."

Charlie zoomed ahead with Jean following him. Rachel and Kirsty were about to join them when they heard a gentle whinny. They looked round and saw a tall white stallion peeping out from a nearby stall.

"What a beautiful horse!" Rachel exclaimed.

The horse whinnied again, and nodded his head a couple of times.

"It's almost as if he's trying to get our attention," said Kirsty. "Come on, let's go and say hello to him."

The nameplate on the horse's stall said "Merlin".

"Hello, Merlin," said Rachel, reaching up and stroking his soft nose.

Then she noticed something strange. "Look, Kirsty!" Rachel said, pointing to the top of Merlin's head. There, as the girls watched, a tiny sparkling light gradually grew brighter, and Princess Anya the Cuddly Creatures Fairy peeked through Merlin's silvery mane!

"Princess Anya!" cried Kirsty in delight.

"Hello, Kirsty! Hello, Rachel," said the Princess Fairy, flashing a dazzling smile and flicking her side plait over her shoulder. She was wearing an orange flippy dress trimmed with animal-print details. "I've come to see how the animals are – I'm pleased to see that my dear friend Merlin seems fine. Have you seen any of the other animals?"

"Yes, we have," said Rachel. "Princess Anya, I think Jack Frost's plan is working! A peacock tried to peck Kirsty's mum's bag, the rabbits didn't want any food, the hens haven't laid any eggs and the guinea pigs are on top of the hen house!"

"And Duchess the pony is in a very bad temper," added Kirsty. "We wondered if it had anything to do with the missing tiaras."

"I'm afraid it does," sighed Anya sadly. "Without my tiara, I can't watch over the special friendship that exists between animals and humans. That's why the animals have been behaving so strangely. I've even had to leave my own little Bengal kitten in Fairyland in case she is affected."

"We have to find that tiara," said Kirsty in a determined voice.

Rachel was feeling puzzled. "Why is Merlin still in a good mood?" she asked Anya.

The fairy's eyes sparkled as she smiled. "He is my special animal friend," she explained. "He's descended from the very first horses that lived at Golden Palace, hundreds of years ago. They carried knights in armour, and Merlin remembers all the stories that have been passed down through his family."

Rachel patted Merlin's warm neck and stroked his silky mane. He gently nuzzled her shoulder.

"It seems as if Merlin is the only animal who still has a special bond with people," Anya said. "Will you take me to see the other animals, girls?"

"Of course," said Kirsty. "You'd better hide, though, Princess Anya."

Rachel held open her jacket pocket so that Anya could fly into it. The girls said goodbye to Merlin and walked towards the petting zoo.

As they drew closer, they heard loud bangs and shouts, and when they reached the zoo, they stared in astonishment.

The five boys they had seen earlier were barging between the animal hutches and pens, shouting out to each other as they ran. Two of them were overturning bales of hay and the others were peering under water troughs and emptying feed buckets. They seemed to be in a panic, and were terrifying the rabbits, guinea pigs and hens, which had all raced into their homes in fright.

Charlie dashed over to the girls, with a sad, worried look on his face.

"Why are those big boys being so mean?" he asked.

"The animals will never be brave enough to come out of their hutches now!"

At that moment, Jean the keeper strode towards the boys, looking very cross. "Leave the zoo at once!" she ordered. "You're upsetting all the animals."

The boys stomped past Rachel and Kirsty, looking very bad-tempered.

"We've got to find it — it must be here somewhere!" the girls heard the tallest boy say.

"What a funny, squawky voice that boy has," Rachel noticed.

"And they all have very big feet for their height…" added Kirsty.

The girls gasped and turned to face each other.

"Kirsty – they're goblins!" Rachel whispered in alarm.

"Yes," said Kirsty. "And it sounds as if they're looking for something. It must be Anya's tiara!"

# Llama Drama

Jean kindly offered to take Charlie to the playground. Rachel and Kirsty were relieved as they needed to speak to Anya, and Charlie wouldn't enjoy the petting zoo while the animals were behaving so strangely.

As soon as Charlie and Jean were out of sight, Anya flew out of Rachel's pocket.

"Those naughty goblins!" Anya exclaimed. "How dare they frighten all the animals like that?"

"At least we know that the tiara is somewhere in the petting zoo," said Kirsty. "The goblins must have dropped it here."

"Quick, let's search for it before they come back," said Rachel eagerly.

"It will be easier for you to look if you're the same size as me," said Anya.

Rachel and Kirsty held hands as Anya waved her wand. A ribbon of glittering gold coiled from the tip of her wand and wound itself into a circle above them. Then it burst like a tiny firework, showering Rachel and Kirsty in silvery sparkles. Instantly, they shrank to fairy size and found themselves hovering beside Anya, fluttering silvery gossamer wings.

The girls started their search in the hen house, where Rachel noticed something immediately.

"The hen in the far corner is sitting on something golden!" she exclaimed. "It *must* be the tiara!"

They zoomed along towards the reddish-brown hen, which clucked at them in surprise.

"Excuse me, do you have my golden tiara?" asked Anya politely.

The hen moved slightly, and the girls saw that she was sitting on a clutch of tiny golden chicks. Although they were very sweet, the girls couldn't help feeling disappointed.

"Let's keep searching," said Anya.

They flew to the goats' enclosure and swooped under the nose of a young billy goat, who glared at them and lowered his head.

"Look out!" cried Rachel as the goat charged at them.

The fairies scattered in three different directions and the billy goat thundered past.

"That was close!" said Kirsty, hovering above the field.

"I don't think the tiara is here," said Princess Anya. "The goblins would have been too scared of that billy goat to enter the enclosure!"

They left the goat still charging around in circles, and fluttered into the rabbit hutches. A soft grey rabbit with fluffy ears stared at them in surprise. Kirsty reached out her hand to touch it, but the rabbit turned tail and jumped into a pile of straw. All the girls could see was its quivering white bobtail.

The girls and Anya searched through the hutches, but all they could find were old lettuce leaves and pieces of straw.

Suddenly a ray of sunshine filtered into the hutch and made something in the far corner flash gold.

"Over here!" cried Kirsty in excitement.

The girls eagerly pulled aside the straw, but all they found was a

chunk of golden-yellow corn.

"It's no use," said Princess Anya, fluttering sadly to the ground. "We'll never find it."

Rachel and Kirsty fluttered down too, and put their arms around the princess's shoulders.

"Don't give up hope," said Rachel.

"We've already found two of the missing tiaras, and we'll find yours too, I promise."

"With all three of us searching, we can't fail," added Kirsty. "Jack Frost is *not* going to get away with this!"

Princess Anya looked more cheerful. "I'm so glad you're here to help me!" she said.

The three fairies fluttered out of the hutch and found themselves in front of the llama pasture. Kirsty gave a cry of surprise as she spotted the five goblins sneaking in through the gate!

50

"Perhaps they've remembered where they lost the tiara," said Rachel. "Come on, let's follow them!"

The three girls zipped along after the goblins, staying close to the ground so that the goblins wouldn't spot them. The llamas were all in one corner, feeding from a large trough.

"Out of my way, Hairy," snapped the tallest goblin, shoving a cream-coloured llama aside.

"Move, Big Neck," shouted a second goblin, who was wearing his riding hat back to front.

He elbowed his way past a chocolate-coloured llama. The other goblins scrambled forward too, plunging their greedy green fingers into the trough and scraping out handfuls of llama grain,. They seemed to be searching to see if anything was at the bottom of the trough.

"Those poor llamas!" said Kirsty under her breath.

"Don't worry," said Princess Anya with a little smile. "Llamas won't stand for being pushed around."

The llamas were already snorting with annoyance. Their food was being trampled into the ground by clumpy

goblin feet! The chocolate-coloured
llama butted one
of the goblins
and sent him
headfirst into
a hedge.

"Help!"
the goblin
squawked
in a muffled
voice. "Get
off me!"

No one went to help him, and the
chocolate-coloured llama bent his head
into the trough. When he lifted it again,
something shining and golden was stuck
on the woolly fur between his ears.

"My tiara!" gasped Princess Anya.

# A Trough and a Tiara

Unfortunately, the goblins had noticed the tiara too.

"GIVE ME THAT!" bawled the tallest of the goblins.

He snatched at it, but the llama gave a loud snort and dashed away from the trough. Alarmed, the other llamas followed him, thundering across the pasture at top speed.

"Catch them!" shouted the goblin. "Stop those horrible hairy beasts!"

The goblins started to chase the llamas, stumbling over weeds and roots. But their squawks and shouts only made the llamas run faster.

"They're too fast for the goblins," said Rachel.

"Yes, but they're too fast for us as well," said Princess Anya. "How can we make them come back?"

The girls thought hard.

"Maybe we could lure them with food?" suggested Kirsty after a moment.

They darted over to the trough, but it was empty.

"Do you remember the sacks that Duchess kicked over, Kirsty?" said Rachel. "Wasn't one of them full of llama grain?"

"Yes!" Kirsty exclaimed. "Well remembered, Rachel. Come on!"

They whizzed out of the pasture, through the petting zoo and into the cobbled yard of the stables.

The sack of llama grain was still there –
but it was a hundred times bigger than
the fairies!

"It's much too heavy for us to carry for
long," said Rachel.

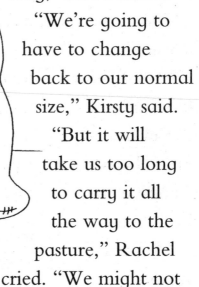

"We're going to
have to change
back to our normal
size," Kirsty said.
"But it will
take us too long
to carry it all
the way to the
pasture," Rachel
cried. "We might not
get back  before the goblins manage to
grab the tiara."

"What are we going to do?" asked
Princess Anya in a panic.

At that moment, a loud neigh echoed through the yard. Merlin's handsome white head was poking out of his stable.

He neighed again, and a big smile spread over Anya's face.

"Of course!" she said. "Merlin wants to help us!"

She touched her wand to the stable door and it sprang open. Merlin trotted out, his shoes clattering over the cobbles.

"Merlin can carry the sack to the pasture in a flash!" said Princess Anya.

"We just have to lift it onto his back."

Rachel and Kirsty each took one
top corner of the sack, and Princess
Anya grabbed the middle. Then, on the
count of three, they all rose into the air,
fluttering their delicate wings as hard as
they could.

"Keep going!" puffed Rachel. "Not –
much – further!"

The bag seemed to get heavier and

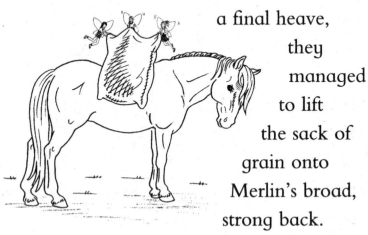

heavier. But at last, with

a final heave,

they

managed

to lift

the sack of

grain onto

Merlin's broad,

strong back.

Then they clung on to his silvery mane
and he was off!

Merlin cantered quickly back through
the petting zoo to the llama pasture.
The surprised faces of goats, pigs and
rabbits were a blur as he raced towards
the pasture fence. Then he gave a loud
whinny.

"Hold on tight!" cried Princess Anya.

The girls wound their tiny hands into
his silky mane,
and Merlin
soared over
the fence.
He landed
on the
soft grass
of the
pasture.

The llamas had gathered together in a corner of the pasture, confronted by four of the goblins, who were all panting and red-faced. The goblins looked very, very cross, but the llamas looked even crosser. They hadn't enjoyed being chased by the goblins, and since Anya didn't have her tiara, they were feeling even grumpier than usual.

As the girls watched, the goblins started to move slowly forward. The llamas began to paw the ground, lowering their woolly heads.

"Those goblins had better watch out," said Rachel. "It looks as if the llamas are about to charge!"

Just as she finished speaking, the llamas hurtled headlong at the goblins – who screeched in terror – and scattered them around the pasture!

"Quickly, Merlin, go up to the llamas!"
said Princess Anya.

Merlin moved towards the llamas,
while Princess Anya, Rachel and Kirsty
pulled open the sack of feed. The llamas
didn't seem to notice them. But then
Anya waved her wand over the food,
sprinkling it with golden
sparkles. A delicious
aroma rose from the
sack, and the llamas
paused, sniffing
the air.

In the distance, the
goblins leaped over
the fence and vanished
from sight.

"Over to the trough,
Merlin!" cried Princess Anya.

Merlin trotted over to the trough, and the girls tipped the grain inside it. Within seconds, the llamas had stuck their heads greedily into the trough. The chocolate-coloured llama was among them, still wearing the golden tiara.

Rachel breathed a huge sigh of relief. They had succeeded! All they needed to do now was to pluck the tiara from the llama's head. But then Kirsty gave a cry of alarm.

The goblin who had been stuck in the hedge had finally wriggled free, and now he was clambering onto the chocolate-coloured llama's back!

# A Royal Result

The llama gave a loud snort and kicked up his back legs, flinging the goblin into the air. The goblin landed on the back of the next llama, who did exactly the same thing – and the next – and the next!

"YOWCH!" squawked the goblin, as he was bounced from llama to llama. "OOOH! OWWW! ARGH!"

Finally he toppled headfirst onto the ground, and lay there panting, spread-eagled in the mud.

As the chocolate-coloured llama dipped his head down to feed again, Rachel gently took the tiara from his woolly head. She handed it to Princess Anya with a big smile.

"We did it!" she said.

Princess Anya took the tiara, and it shrank to fairy size again. She placed it back on top of her golden hair, where it shone as brightly as the sun.

"Girls, I will never forget what you have done for me today," she said, smiling at them. "How can I ever thank you?"

"The best reward is seeing your tiara back where it belongs," said Kirsty, giving Princess Anya a hug. "We're just happy that we found it!"

"Merlin helped too," Rachel reminded her friend.

Princess Anya waved her wand and a large, delicious apple appeared in the air beside Merlin. As he crunched on it happily, Princess Anya waved her wand again, and returned the girls to human size.

"It's time for me to go back to Fairyland," Anya said. "I can't wait to tell the other princesses how wonderful you've been!"

She waved goodbye and then, in a shower of sparkly fairy dust, she was gone. Rachel and Kirsty chatted happily as they led Merlin back to the stables.

"We've done it!" said Rachel. "Three of the missing tiaras have been returned to the princesses!"

"That leaves four still to find," Kirsty added.

"We'll find them," said Rachel in a determined voice. "I know we will!"

As they passed through the petting zoo, they saw Jean scratching her head. The girls hurried up to her.

"All the animals seem happy and friendly again," she said in a surprised voice. "It's as if this morning was just a bad dream. It's like magic!"

The girls shared a secret smile. This meant that Anya's tiara was already restoring the special bond between humans and animals!

"That's wonderful news," said Rachel.

"Charlie is in the playground," said Jean. "I said I would send you to fetch him. I'll take Merlin back to the stable – thanks for giving him a walk, girls!"

When Rachel and Kirsty brought Charlie back to the petting zoo, he was overjoyed that the animals were back to normal. The rabbits let him stroke their soft fur and feed them little titbits. Charlie crouched down and held out a palm full of carrot tops, while hens clucked around his feet. He petted the guinea pigs, fed the goats and even went to see Duchess in her stable. He was a little bit scared that she might knock him over again, but as soon as she saw him, she gave him a friendly nuzzle.

"I think she's saying sorry," said Rachel with a smile.

"You've certainly made a lot of animal friends today, Charlie!" said Kirsty.

At that moment, Jean popped her head around the stable door.

"It's time for today's Kids' Week activity!" she said. "I think you'll enjoy it!"

Kirsty and Rachel walked out of Duchess's stable and stared in delight. Merlin was standing in the middle of the cobbled yard, harnessed to the beautiful carriage they had seen earlier. All the other boys and girls were there too.

"This is a genuine old royal carriage

that has been lovingly restored," Jean
told them. "And Merlin will be pleased
to give everyone a ride in it!"

Rachel and Kirsty
stroked Merlin's
mane and then
climbed into
the carriage.
With a proud

whinny, the horse set off. Rachel sank
back into her soft velvet seat with a
giggle.

"I feel even more like a real princess
than ever!" she said happily.

"Me too!" said Kirsty, gazing out of
the carriage window at the peacocks,
who all looked calm again. "Oh,
Rachel, I can't wait to find out what our
next magical adventure will be!"

Now it's time for Kirsty and
Rachel to help...

# Elisa the Adventure Fairy

**Read on for a sneak peek...**

"I wonder what adventures Louis and
Caroline have arranged for us this
evening," said Kirsty Tate, smiling at her
best friend, Rachel Walker, across the
grand banqueting table.

It was the spring holidays, and they
were staying at Golden Palace for Kids'
Week, a special event for children. Louis
and Caroline were the palace stewards,
and they had been looking after the
children all week as if they were royalty.

"I'm sure they'll have something
wonderful planned," said Rachel,
scraping the last bit of strawberry

ice cream from her silver bowl.

The Banqueting Hall was looking very beautiful, full of twinkling candles and lights. Kirsty gazed thoughtfully out of the large, round window at the end of the hall. It was twilight, but she could see the silhouette of the palace's crumbling old tower.

It rose up majestically from the battlements against the purple sky, and it was the only place that the children were not allowed to go.

"I wish they would let us climb all the way up to the top of the tower," Kirsty said. "I'd love to explore it!"

"It sounds a bit scary to me," said a girl called Victoria, who was sitting next to Kirsty. "I'm not feeling very adventurous."

Rachel and Kirsty exchanged a secret smile. They had already had plenty of adventures that week, helping their friends, the Princess Fairies, get their magic tiaras back from Jack Frost and his goblins. So far they had found the tiaras that belonged to Princess Honor the Happy Days Fairy, Princess Demi the Dressing-Up Fairy and Princess Anya the Cuddly Creatures Fairy. But there were still four more to find...

Read Elisa the Adventure Fairy to find out what adventures are in store for Kirsty and Rachel!

Meet the fairies, play games
and get sneak peeks at
the latest books!

# www.rainbowmagicbooks.co.uk

There's fairy fun for everyone on
our wonderful website.
You'll find great activities, competitions, stories and
fairy profiles, and also a special newsletter.

Get 30% off all Rainbow Magic books at

## www.rainbowmagicbooks.co.uk

Enter the code RAINBOW at the checkout.
Offer ends 31 December 2013.

Offer valid in United Kingdom and Republic of Ireland only.

Look out for the next sparkly
Rainbow Magic Special!

# Robyn the
# Christmas Party Fairy

Rachel and Kirsty are helping to organise a big Christmas party.
But Jack Frost has stolen Robyn the Christmas Party Fairy's
magical objects! The girls must help Robyn,
before the spirit of Christmas is lost forever...

## Out now!

# Alexandra
# the Royal Baby
# Fairy

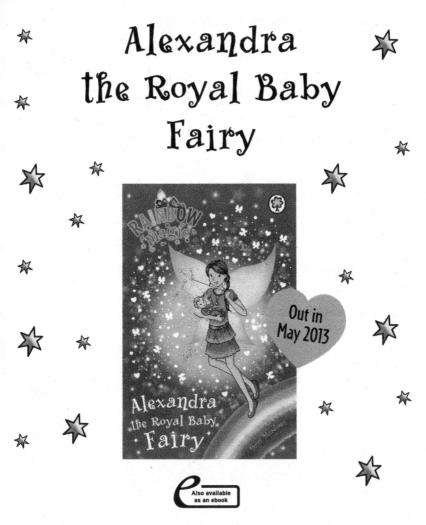

Out in
May 2013

 Also available
as an ebook

The whole of Fairyland is very excited - there's going
to be a new royal baby! But when the special baby
goes missing, Rachel and Kirsty are there to help
their friend, Alexandra the Royal Baby Fairy.

# www.rainbowmagicbooks.co.uk

# Meet the
# Princess Fairies

Honor
the Happy Days
Fairy

Demi
the Dressing-Up
Fairy

Anya
the Cuddly Creatures
Fairy

Elisa
the Adventure
Fairy

Lizzie
the Sweet Treats
Fairy

Maddie
the Playtime
Fairy

Eva
the Enchanted Ball
Fairy

**Jack Frost has stolen the Princess Fairies'
tiaras. Kirsty and Rachel must get them back
before all the magic in the world fades away!**

# www.rainbowmagicbooks.co.uk